E
Shy

DATE DUE

OCT 24 1985	DEC 15 1986	
OCT 31 1985	JAN 6 1987	2B
NOV 14 1985	RE	
SEP 17 1986	3C	DEC 8 1988
NOVAK	MAR 01 1989	3A
	APR 15 1989	KD
NOV 18 1986		
DEC 8 1986		APR 24 19—
		MAY 04 1992
JAN 22 1987		OCT 12 1989
FEB 1987	NOV 27 1989	2D
DEC 13 1989	Griffith	

Stepdog

Stepdog

Marlene Fanta Shyer

Pictures by **Judith Schermer**

Charles Scribner's Sons
New York

Text copyright © 1983 Marlene Fanta Shyer
Illustrations copyright © 1983 Judith Schermer

Library of Congress Cataloging in Publication Data
Shyer, Marlene Fanta.   Stepdog.
Summary: When Terry's dad marries Marilyn, Marilyn's
dog suffers from jealousy.
[1. Remarriage—Fiction. 2. Dogs—Fiction]
I. Schermer, Judith, ill. II. Title.
PZ7.S562St 1983 [E] 83-11649
ISBN 0-684-17998-9

1 3 5 7 9 11 13 15 17 19 W/C 20 18 16 14 12 10 8 6 4 2

Printed in the United States of America.

To Julie Fallowfield
with many thanks for hanging in
M.F.S.

For Mitch
J.S.

The first time I met Dad's friend, Marilyn, she raced me around the block. I won.

The second time I met Marilyn, she brought me a koala bear she'd won in a raffle. "I'll call him Fizzy," I said.

The third time I met Marilyn, she showed me a picture of Hoover. "He shakes hands, runs fast, and can wag his tail at sixty miles an hour," she said.

When Dad told me he was marrying Marilyn, I yelled, "Whoopee!" so loud Dad nearly went through a red light.

That night he showed me slides of his new summer house on Lake Botchawatchee. He said, "I know you'll like it, Terry."

He was right.

He said I would love sleeping in the loft and hiking around the lake in my new hiking shoes.

He was right.

He said, "You'll like Hoover." Was he right?

"Meet your stepdog," Marilyn said to me when I arrived.

"Hello, Hoover," I said, but Hoover would not shake hands or wag his tail. He did not look like his picture, either.

When Marilyn raced me to the lake, Hoover picked up Fizzy and ran with him. Hoover won.

He ran right into the lake with Fizzy. "Fizzy can't swim!" I cried.

Marilyn ordered Hoover to bring Fizzy back. "Be a nice stepdog," she said. Fizzy was soaked, but Hoover did not look sorry.

Later, when we were eating a picnic dinner, Hoover pretended to be sleeping, but he wasn't sleeping. One of my hamburgers disappeared. "That is why I named him Hoover. He picks up everything, like a vacuum cleaner." Marilyn apologized and said she had obviously not fed Hoover enough chow for dinner.

"Maybe he just felt left out," Dad said.

That night, when I climbed into the sleeping loft and was just about to fall asleep, I heard a CRASH. In the light seeping in from the hall I could see Hoover had knocked over the ladder.

I was stuck up in the loft! I yelled until Dad and Marilyn came running and turned on the light. "Hoover, what have you *done*?" Marilyn shook her head and called Hoover naughty while Dad fixed the ladder.

I went to sleep.

The next morning, when we all got up at dawn to go on a hike around the lake, one of my new hiking shoes was missing.

Marilyn looked in the basement. Dad looked on the porch. I looked in all the closets. No one could find it. "I'm sure Hoover picked it up and hid it. I think he's a little jealous. He has never had to share me with a child before," Marilyn said.

"Poor mutt. I guess he can't get used to being a stepdog," Dad said.

Marilyn's face got red when Hoover would not return my shoe. She chained Hoover to his doghouse outside.

When I climbed into the loft that night my eyes stayed open. I heard Hoover crying outside.

I looked out the window. Hoover looked lonely. He also looked sorry. "Don't cry, Hoover," I said, through the window. Hoover stopped crying, but I still tossed and turned.

"You'll get used to being a stepdog. I'm not mad at you," I said when I went down and unchained him.

Hoover wagged his tail at sixty miles an hour and followed me into the house. He curled up under the loft. He did not knock over the ladder. I went to sleep.

I dreamed I turned into a dog just like Hoover. I couldn't talk. I couldn't ask for a hamburger. I couldn't tell anyone my feelings were hurt. In my dream no one came to my doghouse to kiss me good-night.

When I woke up, I was glad I was me. My shoe was back and so was a pile of others, a whole bunch, like a big bouquet of boots, sneakers, and sandals.

I put my arms around Hoover's neck and I hugged and hugged. "Thank you, Hoover. I know it's not easy to be a stepdog," I said. Hoover licked my ear.

"Now that Hoover has picked up every shoe in the house, we might as well each find a pair and go on our hike!" Dad said.

"I'll race you all to the lake," Marilyn said. I won. Hoover came in second.

Dad said he knew I'd like my stepdog. He was right.